A Star Witness

Don't miss the other

Nancy Drew
Clue Books:

Pool Party Puzzler
Last Lemonade Standing

Nancy Drew

* CLUE BOOK *

#3

A Star Witness

BY CAROLYN KEENE * ILLUSTRATED BY PETER FRANCIS

Aladdin

NEW YORK   LONDON   TORONTO   SYDNEY   NEW DELHI

ALADDIN

An imprint of Simon & Schuster Children's Publishing Division
1230 Avenue of the Americas, New York, New York 10020
First Aladdin paperback edition November 2015
Text copyright © 2015 by Simon & Schuster, Inc.
Illustrations copyright © 2015 by Peter Francis
Also available in an Aladdin hardcover edition.
All rights reserved, including the right of reproduction in whole or in part in any form.
ALADDIN is a trademark of Simon & Schuster, Inc., and related logo is a
registered trademark of Simon & Schuster, Inc.
NANCY DREW, NANCY DREW CLUE BOOK, and colophons
are registered trademarks of Simon & Schuster, Inc.
For information about special discounts for bulk purchases, please contact Simon & Schuster
Special Sales at 1-866-506-1949 or business@simonandschuster.com.
The Simon & Schuster Speakers Bureau can bring authors to your live event.
For more information or to book an event contact the Simon & Schuster Speakers Bureau at
1-866-248-3049 or visit our website at www.simonspeakers.com.
Designed by Karina Granda
The illustrations for this book were rendered digitally.
The text of this book was set in Adobe Garamond Pro.
Manufactured in the United States of America 1015 OFF
2 4 6 8 10 9 7 5 3 1
Library of Congress Control Number 2014954566
ISBN 978-1-4814-3998-5 (hc)
ISBN 978-1-4814-3750-9 (pbk)
ISBN 978-1-4814-3751-6 (eBook)

✳ CONTENTS ✳

Chapter

1

SPACE AND BEYOND

"That's it! That's them!" George Fayne cried as Mr. Drew pulled up outside the planetarium. She pointed out the car window. A group of people of all different ages was standing near the entrance. A woman with glasses and frizzy red hair held up a green flag with the letters RHAC written on it.

"That's the River Heights Astronomy Club?" Nancy Drew asked, looking at the group in front of them. There was a woman wearing a turtleneck (even though it was eighty degrees out), standing with a little girl a few years younger than Nancy, and a couple with white hair. It wasn't quite what she'd expected.

"Yup! Those are my friends Marty and Hilda," George said, hopping out of the car and pointing to the white-haired couple. "Hilda makes great banana bread. And that's Trina. She's the youngest member—only five. And her mom, Celia." George pointed at the woman in the turtleneck. "Thanks for the ride, Mr. Drew!"

Carson Drew smiled as he watched his daughter, Nancy, and her friends Bess Marvin and George climb the stairs to the entrance. "You girls have a great time today," he said. "I'll be back later to pick you up."

"Right after we see the Starship 5000!" George said.

"What's the Starship 5000?" Bess whispered to Nancy.

Nancy just shrugged. George and Bess were cousins, but they couldn't have been more different. George loved adventure. She went hiking on the weekends, was part of their town's astronomy club and their school's chess club, and was the first of their friends to try judo. She wore her brown hair short and only went to the mall when her mom made her go back-to-school shopping—or to buy another electronic gadget to add to her collection. Her cousin Bess liked spending nights curled up on the couch, watching old movies. She had wavy blond hair that went past her shoulders and had the perfect outfit for every occasion— whether it was a school dance or the state fair.

"How many meetings have you been to so far?" Bess asked as they walked toward the group.

"This will be my fourth," George said over her shoulder. "And the best—obviously. At most meetings we just eat donuts in the library and talk about stars and stuff. I haven't been to the planetarium since first grade!"

Nancy looked up at the giant white building in front of them. There was a dome on one side— that was where they held all the different space shows. She'd passed it so many times, but hadn't been inside since she was in first grade either. Now that George had joined the River Heights Astronomy Club, they finally had a reason to go back. George had been talking about the big trip for over two weeks now. The club was going to explore the museum and see a special show by a famous astronomer, Dr. Arnot, in the dome. George had invited Bess and Nancy along as her special guests.

"George! You made it!" The woman with the red hair checked something off her clipboard as the three girls climbed the stairs. "And you brought your friends. Delightful!"

The white-haired man named Marty smiled. "You must be Nancy and Bess!" he said, looking at them. "George has told us all about you."

Hilda peered over her tiny wire glasses. She pointed to Bess. "Aren't you two cousins?"

"Yup," George said.

"And you and Nancy have that club together," Marty said. "Solving mysteries."

"Something like that," Nancy said. She glanced

sideways at George and smiled. Nancy, Bess, and George had a club called the Clue Crew. They'd become good at helping people in River Heights figure out things they couldn't on their own. Sometimes someone's cell phone disappeared. Other times the Clue Crew found lost dogs. One time they'd helped Nancy's neighbor after her prize-winning roses were stolen. Nancy even had a special Clue Book she used to write down important details and suspects.

"George! You're here!" the little girl, Trina, called out. She ran over to George and gave her a big hug. She was dressed in black boots and a little green hat with a bow on it, and carried around a tiny pair of binoculars. Trina's mom smiled as George picked Trina up and spun her around.

"Wouldn't miss it!" George said. When she put Trina down, George turned to Nancy and Bess. "I taught Trina everything she knows about the Milky Way."

The red-haired woman patted Nancy on the back. She was older than Nancy's dad, and every inch of her skin was covered with freckles. "We're happy to have you girls. I'm Lois Oslo, the head of the astronomy club. As George might've told you, this is our sixth annual visit to the museum. Let's begin, shall we?"

She waved the green flag in the air as she turned inside. There were only seven astronomy club members besides Lois, so the flag didn't seem necessary, but Nancy followed along anyway.

When they stepped into the museum's front entrance, Nancy grabbed George's arm. "Wow! I'd forgotten how amazing it is."

They stood there, staring up at the fifty-foot ceiling. It was painted a deep blue with tiny glittering white stars. "I think I see the Big Dipper!" Bess said, pointing to the constellation that looked like a cooking pot with a big handle.

"You're correct," Marty said. Then he moved Bess's hand so she was pointing at a different cluster of stars in the sky. These looked like a smaller pot—one that you'd cook macaroni and cheese in. "And that's the Little Dipper."

"Yes, the entranceway is impressive," Lois said, pushing to the right, past a group of kids wearing Driftwood Day Camp T-shirts. "But not as impressive as the Hall of Planets."

They followed Lois into a room that had one long glass wall. Floating in front of the wall were each of the eight planets. Some of the planets had been hollowed out and were big enough to walk around in. People were climbing the stairs and wandering inside them, reading different information about Saturn or Jupiter.

Trina hovered next to her mom, pointing at each planet one by one. "My very easy method just speeds up names," she said slowly.

"I remember that!" Bess laughed. "Isn't that how we learned what order they go in?"

"That's right," Nancy said, going down the row. "Mercury, Venus, Earth . . ."

"Mars, Jupiter, Saturn, Uranus, and Neptune," Lois finished. "Very good, girls! Now let's take a half hour or so in here to look around, shall we?"

The group split apart, with Celia and Trina going straight for Jupiter. There was a window in the giant planet's side, right where its great red spot is. Nancy and Bess followed George to Earth. They climbed the stairs that wrapped around the planet and went inside the back. There were even seats so they could sit down.

A booming voice came out of the speakers. "Four and a half billion years ago, Earth was formed. It's known by many names: Terra . . . Gaia . . . the world. This, the third planet from the sun, is the only celestial body proven to accommodate life."

A screen on one of the walls showed videos of people from all different countries. One woman was weaving a basket and another was carrying pineapples on her back. There were scenes of panda bears and strange colorful insects, followed by underwater scenes of sharks and dolphins.

Nancy and her friends watched the entire video, then went on to Mars, reading a sign about the different rovers, or vehicles, that had landed on the planet's surface. They visited Jupiter and Saturn before noticing Lois and the rest of the group waiting by the exit. "We'll have more time at the end of the day!" Lois called. "I promise. But right now we should go see the north wing of the building, where there is a new asteroid exhibit."

Marty and Hilda waited for the girls to catch up. The group was almost out of the Hall of

Planets when they noticed an older man with wiry gray hair that stuck up in different directions. He wore a polka-dotted orange bow tie and had what looked like a mustard stain on his shirt collar. The man was standing in the hallway, talking loudly to a young woman who was wearing black-rimmed glasses and a red headband. She had on black Mary Jane shoes.

"Creepin' conundrums!" the man cried. "I can't believe that security guard nearly didn't let us into the museum. I forgot my ID today, so I spent twenty minutes trying to convince him I was who I said I was, and then I had to ask to speak to the planetarium director. I mean, really—you'd have thought I was trying to bring some wild hyenas in here! It was just a telescope!"

The young woman turned, noticing Lois and the rest of the group standing behind them. Lois smiled and waved at her. They must've known each other. "Dr. Arnot!" the young woman said. "This is the River Heights Astronomy Club! They're coming to your space show tonight.

Remember, I had told you about them?"

Dr. Arnot turned around, looking confused. It was clear he didn't remember.

Lois stuck out her hand. "Dr. Arnot!" she said. "I'm Lois Oslo. What an honor. I've watched your TV specials since I was a teenager. *Space and Beyond* is my favorite. Thank you so much for hosting us tonight; it's a special day for our club."

Dr. Arnot puffed up his chest and smiled. "Well, it is a pleasure to meet you too. I was just telling Kirsten here, I brought the Starship 5000—one of the most high-tech telescopes—on loan from an astronomer in Germany. Only one was ever made. The lens is more powerful than any other in the world. So you'll be getting a special treat tonight on the museum's roof. Now, if you'll excuse me, I have to find the director of the planetarium. We have a few things to discuss."

The man turned and disappeared down the hall. Kirsten smiled at the group. Nancy noticed she was sipping a grape soda. She'd been hiding it behind her when she was talking to Dr. Arnot.

Nancy remembered seeing a sign posted near the museum's entrance that said food and beverages were not allowed, so she figured that Kirsten probably didn't want Dr. Arnot to see her drinking in the museum. "I'm Kirsten Levy," she said, introducing herself. "Dr. Arnot's assistant. I'm so happy you're all here."

Lois beamed at the club's members. "I e-mailed Kirsten months back, and she was kind enough to arrange the special telescope viewing for us. Such a sweetheart!"

"So how long have you been working with Dr. Arnot?" Marty asked.

"For a year now," Kirsten said, and then she quickly finished the last of her soda. "He's very busy with travel and filming his TV show, so I help out when he's in town. I'm studying astronomy at River Heights Community College."

"Cool," Trina said. "So you want to be an astro . . . nomer?" She had trouble getting out the whole word.

"Yeah, I think so," Kirsten said. She pushed

her glasses up on her nose. "I love studying the stars. I'm actually part of a group project at school researching the Andromeda Galaxy. We're supposed to be presenting to the class tonight, but since I'm working here, my friend is going to cover for me."

"Oh, we'd hate to keep you from your presentation!" Hilda said.

Kirsten just shook her head. "No, this is one of my favorite parts of my job with Dr. Arnot. I love showing groups the night sky. He does an amazing planetarium show too. I think you'll really love it."

"We're going to explore the museum until the show tonight," George said. "What's your favorite thing here?"

"Have you seen the moon landing exhibit?" Kirsten asked.

George raised her eyebrows at Nancy and Bess. "A moon landing exhibit? That sounds awesome!"

Kirsten waved for the group to follow her. They went down a side hallway that led to a smaller room. The floor was grayish white with fake craters all over it. The walls were painted black with glittering stars. On one wall you could see Earth.

"It's just like we're on the moon," Bess remarked.

Nancy climbed on top of the replica of the moon rover. "Look!" she cried, picking up an astronaut's helmet. "They even have costumes."

Kirsten smiled. "I'm off to find Dr. Arnot. Enjoy the museum! We'll see you tonight!"

The rest of the group scattered. Some studied the

text on the wall beside the rover, which described the first time a human landed on the moon in 1969. Nancy and her friends put on the astronaut helmets. There were even puffy astronaut jackets that were all white with different metallic pieces on them. The girls put those on too.

"I can barely see out of this," Bess said with a giggle. She almost fell back over the side of the moon rover, but George grabbed her hand, keeping her steady.

Nancy climbed down off the rover, grabbing the flag that was there for a prop. She pretended to walk very slowly, like she was moving through water. She'd seen the footage of the first moon landing in science class. Buzz Aldrin had floated and bounced above the surface of the moon.

Then, with Marty and Hilda watching, she took her first step. Lois and two women standing nearby clapped. "One small step for man," Nancy said, some of astronaut Neil Armstrong's words echoing inside her helmet, "one giant leap for mankind!"

Chapter

A STAR-STUDDED SHOW

"What do you think?" Nancy asked, studying her friends' faces. "Does it look like us?"

Bess and George stared at the picture on the table in front of them. They'd found a man in the garden outside the Hall of Comets who was drawing caricatures of different kids. He'd even drawn the group of Driftwood Day Campers that Nancy had noticed earlier. When Bess, George, and Nancy sat down in front of him, he'd drawn them floating through space in astronaut suits.

They were holding hands with the Earth in the background.

"I think so," George said. "But our heads are three times bigger than our bodies in this drawing!"

"They're supposed to be that way," Bess said. "It's a caricature—a cartoon version of us."

"I hope my head never looks that big in real life," George muttered, shaking her head.

"Well, I think you all look amazing!" Marty said, leaning over to study the drawing. Nancy, Bess, and George were sitting with the rest of the astronomy club at the café, which overlooked the Hall of Comets. A giant model of Halley's Comet was right behind them.

Bess took a bite of the ice-cream sandwich on the plate in front of her and made a face. "Wait, what's wrong with this? It doesn't taste like ice cream. It's . . . dry!"

"It's astronaut ice cream," Hilda explained. "The kind they send to space. It's dehydrated, which means all the moisture has been taken out so you can eat it even in zero gravity."

"I love it!" Trina declared as she finished hers.

"It's yummy," Nancy agreed. She took another bite, letting the crispy chocolate cracker melt in her mouth before swallowing it down.

"All right, everyone!" Lois called, pushing her chair back from the table. "The big star show starts in five minutes. Is everyone ready to listen to world famous astronomer Dr. Arnot talk about space?"

"I sure am!" Celia said. Her black turtleneck even had a star pinned to the collar.

Nancy and the rest of the group followed Lois through the museum. Lois was still holding the green flag, waving it whenever the halls got too crowded. They climbed a flight of stairs and ended up right outside the giant dome. Kirsten was standing by the door.

"You made it!" she said with a smile. "Come in and have a seat wherever you'd like. Dr. Arnot will be here in a few minutes."

"Let's sit in the back," George suggested, moving down one of the auditorium's last rows. She plopped into one of the seats and leaned her head back, gazing at the dome above. "I remember this from when we were in first grade. Field trips here were the coolest."

"Didn't they make it rain in here somehow?" Bess asked, staring up at the ceiling.

"That's right!" Nancy said. "They used to have thunderstorms at the end of the show."

She was about to remind them about the field trip when Deirdre Shannon stood up and screamed as the water came down from the ceiling, but then the lights in the dome went out. Music blasted from a speaker on the wall. In the dim glow, Nancy could just make out Dr. Arnot walking in from the back of the room.

"So cool!" George said under her breath. The ceiling was now covered with stars.

"Thirteen point eight billion years ago there was a giant explosion called the Big Bang," Dr. Arnot began. "In that moment everything we know—all matter and energy—was born, including the sun, the moon, the stars, and Earth."

The picture on the ceiling changed, showing all the planets in the solar system, along with the sun. Dr. Arnot continued, describing how the planets were formed. Then he talked about the different types of life on Earth and how they all came from the same place.

Nancy and her friends kept their heads tilted back, staring up at the show on the ceiling. Dr. Arnot told them about the age of the dinosaurs, and the meteor that had crashed and caused their extinction. As he spoke, different images flashed across the ceiling. There was a giant Tyrannosaurus rex and a Stegosaurus. Then the pictures showed how certain animals may have evolved from the dinosaurs.

It had only been an hour, but Dr. Arnot had gone through nearly the whole history of the planet Earth. Then the dome changed so that it looked like the night sky, and Dr. Arnot pointed out different clusters of stars. There was Leo the lion, Pegasus, and Pisces the fish. The grand finale was the thunderstorm, just like Nancy remembered.

Thunder cracked and lightning streaked across the dome. Then, just like magic, water came down from the ceiling. A few rows in front of them, Trina held her hands up to the sky. "How do they do that, Mom?" she asked, laughing. "It's really raining!"

When it was finished, Nancy and her friends stood and clapped. "We haven't even gotten to the best part!" Dr. Arnot called out. The lights came on, and he led the group to one of the side doors. "Now we go up to the roof to do a little star gazing. This is where the Starship 5000 comes in handy. I own a few telescopes myself, but there's only one Starship 5000 in the entire world! It's such a special instrument." He gazed into the distance, and Nancy thought he looked like he might cry with joy.

"Dr. Arnot sure loves that telescope," she whispered to Bess as they all climbed the stairs.

"Can you blame him?" Bess asked. "It sounds totally cool!"

"I read all about the Starship 5000 in *Star*

Shine magazine," Lois said once they reached the top. "It's the best way to observe far-off galaxies, isn't it?"

"It's very precise," Dr. Arnot agreed. He stepped out onto the roof, the astronomy club following close behind him. "You can see Saturn and Jupiter up close and personal! A magnificent sight if you haven't seen them through a scope yet."

"I have, but I don't think George has," Lois said. "She's the group's newest member."

"We haven't either!" Marty said a little too loudly. He fiddled with his ear, adjusting his hearing aid.

Nancy and her friends walked over to the far corner of the roof, leaning over the short wall and staring out across River Heights. From up high they could see everything: the town hall, Main Street with a dozen shops and restaurants, and even the amusement park.

"Look! Our school!" Nancy said, pointing to a white building several blocks over.

Bess squinted at a house down the street. "Is that your—"

"Where is it?" Dr. Arnot yelped. He turned around, scanning the length of the roof. He checked behind Marty, as if the old man might be hiding something behind his back. "The telescope—it's gone!"

"Now, now, Dr. Arnot," Kirsten said. "Maybe someone brought it downstairs. It's probably just a misunderstanding."

Dr. Arnot's face turned pale. "Misunderstanding, fishunderstanding!" he cried, holding his head in his hands. "Call security—quick. Someone must've stolen it!"

Chapter

A PLANET-SIZE PANIC

Three security guards ran onto the roof. Nancy and her friends stood there with the rest of the group, watching as the guards searched every inch of the place, looking under benches and by the emergency exit stairs.

"Creepin' conundrums! Kirsten and I moved it here just before the planetarium show. That couldn't have been more than an hour ago," Dr. Arnot said, looking at one of the guards. "I thought someone was watching it!"

A heavier man with a white mustache scratched his head. "I *was* guarding it. . . . I don't know what happened. I was standing right by the entrance to the roof," he said, staring at the ground. "I only let one group of people up while you were in the show."

"I checked on it once too," a redheaded guard added. "I was down near the Hall of Planets at the bottom of the stairs. When I looked twenty minutes ago, it was still here."

Dr. Arnot put his face in his hands. "It's not like it has legs. It couldn't have just gotten up and walked away."

"Now, calm down," the third security guard said. He was tall and thin, with spiky blond hair. Nancy noticed he was wearing a name tag that read STEVE. "It has to be here somewhere." He turned to the man with the mustache. "That group you let up here . . . who were they?"

The man shrugged. "They're a group from River Heights Greens Retirement Home that comes here every week. They are all women. A bit older."

"My grandma lives at River Heights Greens!" Trina jumped in. Her mom nodded.

"My friends Margie and Greta live there too," Hilda said, and sat down next to Marty on one of the benches.

Dr. Arnot started pacing the length of the roof. "Do you think they took it? It *is* quite valuable. Not to mention, beautiful," he added.

"I watched a bunch of them come down the stairs," the redheaded guard said, "and I didn't see anyone with a telescope."

"They were probably hiding it," Dr. Arnot said, wringing his hands. "I do hope it's all right."

Kirsten walked around the roof, checking under some of the benches, even though the guards had looked there already. She peered over the roof's short wall and then returned to the group. "It's like it completely vanished!"

"We'll start searching the rest of the museum," Steve said, ushering the other two to the exit. "It has to be somewhere. Don't worry, we'll find it."

But as soon as the guards went down the stairs,

the door falling shut behind them, Dr. Arnot shook his head. "This is terrible!"

Lois sat down beside him. "There are still a few hours before the museum closes," she said. "Hopefully they'll turn up something soon."

"Whoever took it might already be gone," Dr. Arnot said. "And that telescope is valuable! How can I go back to Igor and tell him I've lost it?"

Lois's eyes widened. "Igor Perchensky lent it to you? The famous German astronomer?"

That didn't seem to make Dr. Arnot feel better. When he looked up, his eyes were red. "Yes, Igor Perchensky!" he cried. "That's exactly who. It was his telescope. Tell me, how is anyone going to take me seriously after this? Everyone will know I lost it. I'll no longer be known as Dr. Arnot, world famous astronomer. I'll just be Dr. Guy-who-lost-the-very-important-and-special-telescope-and-should-never-be-trusted-ever-again."

"That doesn't have such a great ring to it, does it?" Bess whispered to Nancy.

Nancy looked at Dr. Arnot. His gray hair was a

mess, and his bow tie was crooked. It was hard not to feel bad for him.

"What do you think?" Bess hissed to Nancy and George.

"I think the Clue Crew has our next case," Nancy answered. She didn't look away from Dr. Arnot. He was telling Lois how he had finally become friends with Igor, an astronomer he'd admired for years. Now it would all be ruined.

"Let's get to it," Nancy said, already glancing around the roof for clues. She knew they didn't have much time. They had to find their suspect— whoever it was—fast. There were only three hours left before the museum closed and the telescope would be gone . . . forever!

Chapter

4

A PRIME SUSPECT

Nancy walked up to Dr. Arnot and pulled the Clue Book from her bag. She always kept it there in case she needed to write down clues or leads on unsolved cases. "Dr. Arnot," she said, "do you have any idea who would've done this?"

Dr. Arnot threw up his hands. "Anyone who wanted an expensive telescope," he said. "This one is worth more than five hundred thousand dollars."

Kirsten shook her head. "But not many people know that," she said. "Someone might have just taken it because they thought it looked cool."

"Well, I can't imagine it was anyone from River Heights Greens," Hilda spoke up with a frown. "They wouldn't do something like that."

Nancy wrote down "Motives" at the top of a page. It was just another word for why someone would commit a crime. She wrote everything she could think of underneath it.

Motives:
Wanted to sell the telescope
Wanted it for themselves
Thought it looked cool

"Was there anyone suspicious walking around today?" Bess asked. "Anyone who looked like they might be up to something?"

Dr. Arnot seemed to think for a

moment and then shook his head. "Not that I can remember."

George perked up. "What about that security guard? You were talking about him when we first saw you near the Hall of Planets. You'd said you'd gotten into an argument with him."

"Oh! Him!" Dr. Arnot said. "Yes, very rude fellow."

Kirsten clasped her hands together. "We were bringing the telescope in through the museum's side entrance," she said. "And he yelled at us. He was very annoyed that we didn't go through the front door."

Dr. Arnot puffed up his chest, impersonating the guard. "He said, 'Who do you think *you* are? What do you think *you're* doing?'"

"We explained to him we were just bringing it inside," Kirsten continued, "but he was really angry."

"I told him who I was," Dr. Arnot said, "and explained that I'd forgotten my ID. Then I asked to speak with the planetarium director, but that only made him angrier. He thought I was threatening him. I just wanted to bring the telescope indoors safely!"

"What did the guard do?" Bess twisted her thick blond hair into a ponytail as she spoke.

"His face got quite red—like a tomato!— and then he told me I'd be sorry," Dr. Arnot said.

George glanced sideways at Nancy. "Are you thinking what I'm thinking?" she whispered.

"Prime suspect," Nancy said, flipping the page of the Clue Book to write down the new information.

Suspects:
Security guard

"Can you tell us what he looked like?" Bess asked. "Do you remember his name?"

"He was a short fellow," Dr. Arnot said. "No more than five foot six. He was bald except for a tuft of blond hair in the center of his head. I can't remember his name, though. I don't think he had a name tag on."

Nancy wrote down the description in the Clue Book. "Do you remember anything else?"

Dr. Arnot sighed. "I think he had blue eyes and a little goatee on his chin."

"We shouldn't overlook other possible suspects," George said. "It might have been someone from River Heights Greens. They were up here last."

Hilda shook her head. "I don't think that's right. Why would any of those ladies want an expensive telescope? Plus, most of them are old and small. They would have trouble even carrying it down the stairs!"

Nancy wrote down "River Heights Greens," but she knew it was unlikely. Hilda was right. Most older women wouldn't be able to carry a telescope down the stairs without being noticed by security. Still, Nancy's father, who was a lawyer, had always told her she shouldn't judge a suspect by his or her looks.

"We have to look at anyone who might've been involved," Bess said. "It helps to be thorough."

"Someone might've wanted to steal it and sell it for money," George added.

"But someone's grandma?" Marty asked. "Do you really think that's likely?"

Nancy glanced at her friends. She didn't think it was likely. Not at all.

Nancy, Bess, and George moved away from the group to discuss the case. Bess looked down at the Clue Book in Nancy's hand, pointing to the person listed at the top: security guard. "He's the one with a real motive. If he was angry after his fight with Dr. Arnot, he may have taken the telescope as revenge."

"But there must be two dozen security guards in the museum," George said, "and we don't have a name. What do you want to do, just wander around trying to find him?"

Nancy shrugged. "We could cover the place in an hour," she said.

The girls looked at one another, knowing it

would be a risk. If they couldn't find the suspect, or if it took them a full hour to find him, that would be time they could've spent searching for clues. They weren't even sure he was the one who did it. They only had a hunch—a feeling about him.

"It's the only lead we have so far," Bess said. "So let's track him down and see what happens."

Nancy and George nodded in agreement. "You're right," Nancy said.

The girls said good-bye to Dr. Arnot and the rest of the group and then hurried down the stairs.

Chapter

BREAK ROOM BUST!

"Didn't we just pass that asteroid?" Bess asked with a groan, looking up at the giant black rock hanging from the ceiling. "I swear that's the third time we've seen it."

Nancy spun around, staring at the comets on the other end of the atrium. The café was still bustling with people, some eating the last of their astronaut ice cream. "I don't know," she said. "I thought we were going the right way, but now I'm not so sure."

They'd been searching the museum for almost thirty minutes, going through every hall and exhibit, looking for the guard. They hadn't found him anywhere. When they'd asked another guard if he'd seen anyone who fit the description, he'd gotten confused. "What do you mean he has a puff of blond hair in the center of his head?" he'd asked. "That's so odd!" Then the guard had chuckled and walked away.

Now they were near the café, which they'd

already passed three times. They couldn't figure out how to get into the other half of the museum. "I thought it was that way." George pointed to an exit along the far wall. "Or did we come from over there?"

Nancy noticed a crowd on the other side of the atrium, beyond the café. It took her a moment to realize what it was. The artist who'd drawn them earlier was still there, making caricatures of more people.

"I have an idea!" Nancy said, starting toward him and motioning for Bess and George to follow. "We can have the caricature artist draw a picture of our suspect. That way we'll have something to show people when we're looking for him. It might help us find him faster."

Once they'd arrived, Nancy explained everything to the artist, whose name was Christo. She told him that he should draw a man who was five foot six, wore a security guard's uniform, and had a blond goatee. She even described his tuft of hair. Christo leaned over the drawing, working on the man's face. When Christo was finally done he spun the drawing around. "What do you think? Does this look like him?"

Bess stared at the picture of the man in the security uniform. "It definitely looks like the guard Dr. Arnot described. Maybe it will be enough to help us find him."

"Ahhhhh," Christo said. "So you don't know him, but you're trying to find him. Well, if he works here, the break room might be a good place to start."

"The break room? Where's that?" George asked. She turned, scanning the café for anything they might have missed.

"It's actually right behind the café," Christo said, pointing to a door. "It's where all the museum employees hang out when we have fifteen minutes or so. I think I saw a few guards walking in there not too long ago."

Nancy raised an eyebrow. Now that they had the drawing, it would be easier to find the mysterious guard who'd threatened Dr. Arnot. All they had to do was ask around and show the picture. Surely someone knew him. "And he doesn't look familiar to you?"

Christo shook his head. "I haven't seen him before."

Bess walked toward the break room. "Thank you!" she called over her shoulder. "You've been a huge help."

Nancy and George followed her. Nancy held the drawing in her hands. When they got to a door that read EMPLOYEES ONLY, Bess didn't even knock. She just opened the door and slipped inside. Nancy and George shuffled in after her.

The room they stepped into had a large table with chairs around it, and a hallway off the back that looked like it led to a kitchen. Two women in security uniforms were talking over turkey sandwiches. "She told me the red highlights would be best with my skin tone," a woman with a short red bob was saying. She paused when she noticed the three girls standing by the door.

"Excuse us for interrupting, but we were hoping you could help us with something," Bess said.

Nancy held up the picture of the security guard. "Does this guard look familiar? We wanted to ask him some questions."

The red-haired woman, who had a name tag that said ALMA, laughed. "Well, what do you know? That is one funny picture of Bill. Look at how big his head is!"

The other woman, whose name tag said LOUISE, smiled. "Hey, Bill!" she called into the kitchen. "Some kids are looking for you!"

The man stepped into the room, scratching his bald head. Nancy could immediately smell his cologne—it was like a jar of oregano. "Me? Who's looking for me?"

Nancy rolled up the picture in her hands. "We were hoping to ask you a few questions," she said, "about where you were about an hour and a half ago."

The man's face went pale. "What do you mean?"

"A very expensive telescope disappeared from the roof of the museum," Bess explained. "The astronomer Dr. Arnot was borrowing it from a scientist in Germany. We have good reason to think someone stole it."

The man shook his head. Nancy noticed he wasn't looking at them when he spoke. That was always suspicious! "I didn't have anything to do with that," he said.

"Did you see Dr. Arnot bringing the telescope into the building earlier today?" George asked. "He told us you yelled at him."

"What does it matter?" the man said, pushing past them to the door. "I told you I had nothing to do with that telescope disappearing. Besides, I don't have to explain myself to a bunch of kids. Now if you'll excuse me, I have a job to do."

He stormed out of the room, letting the door

fall shut behind him. Nancy stared at Bess and George with her mouth open in surprise. "He wouldn't even look at us," she whispered.

"I know," Bess said. "He's definitely hiding something."

George and Nancy went to the door, peering into the café. Bill was weaving in and out of tables. He started down the Hall of Comets and disappeared into the east wing of the museum.

"Yeah," Nancy said. "But what?"

Chapter

CAUGHT ON CAMERA

Alma followed the girls to the door, watching Bill go. "If I explain what's going on with him," Alma said, "you have to promise not to tell our boss."

George's eyes widened. "How can we promise that? If he took the telescope—"

"He didn't take the telescope," Alma interrupted. She walked into the kitchen of the break room, gesturing for the girls to follow her. Once they were there, she stared at the soda machine and finally pushed the top button. A can fell to the bottom with a clanking sound. She picked up the orange soda and opened it, taking a sip.

"If he didn't take it, does he know who did?" Nancy asked.

Alma glanced over the girls' shoulders at Louise, who had followed them into the kitchen. Louise was tall and had curly black hair.

"All right," Alma finally said, as if she was just deciding to tell them Bill's secret. "I don't know anything about that missing telescope, and I don't think Bill does either. But you girls were right— he *was* hiding something."

"He switched with someone for his last shift," Louise said. "We're not allowed to do that, but he wanted to work outside the café. He was supposed to be working in the Hall of Planets, though."

"Why did he need to switch?" George asked.

Alma laughed. "Well, you see, Bill has a little crush on Polly, one of the waitresses in the café. She only works on Saturdays, so one of his friends switched with him. He worked in the café and his friend went to the Hall of Planets. And Bill got to make googly eyes at Polly for two hours." She rolled her eyes.

"Two hours?" Nancy asked. She had pulled out the Clue Book and was writing down everything the guards said. "Which two hours? Are you sure he was there the entire time?"

Alma took another sip of her orange soda. "Hmm . . . must've been from four to six p.m. He just got off his shift."

George leaned over, looking at the Clue Book notes. "We went to the show from four to five," she told Nancy. "And Dr. Arnot had brought the telescope up to the roof just before that. So it must've been stolen in that hour window."

The other guard pushed through the kitchen to a door on the other side. She waved at the girls to follow her. "If you want to see for yourself, come on."

Nancy and her friends went into the room with Alma and Louise. There was another guard in there, sitting at a desk covered with computer

monitors. Each monitor showed a different part of the museum.

"Security cameras!" Bess said, pulling up a seat. "Why didn't you say something sooner? All we have to do is look at video of the roof and we'll know who took the telescope."

Alma sat down beside her. "There's only one problem. There is no security camera on the roof. What do you think, Paul? Can you pull up the four o'clock shift near the café?"

Alma looked to the guard on her other side, a gray-haired man with a mustache and glasses. He hit a few buttons on his keyboard and the main monitor showed the café. The time said 4:01 p.m.

"You're right," George said, pointing to the screen. "That's Bill, right there!"

Nancy narrowed her eyes, studying the black-and-white video. Sure enough, Bill was standing against a wall by the café. He kept looking and making silly faces at the waitress who was serving a table a few feet away.

"Can you speed it up so we can see the whole two-hour shift?" Alma asked.

"That would help," Nancy agreed. "Just so we can be one hundred percent certain he never left that spot."

Paul nodded. He hit a button on the keyboard to fast-forward the footage. Nancy could see Bill in the video. He shifted on his feet. At one point he checked his cell phone. But for the whole two hours he just stood there, giving visitors directions or waving to Polly.

"See?" Alma said when it was finally done. "I told you. He's not your suspect."

"He has an alibi," Nancy said. She'd learned that word while the Clue Crew had been solving other mysteries. An alibi was when someone was in another place at the time a crime happened. It proved that they weren't a suspect.

"If he's not our thief," Bess said, "then who is?"

Nancy flipped through the Clue Book, stopping at the page where she'd written down the list of suspects. There was only one other group of people they hadn't yet talked to. "The women from River Heights Greens."

"You really think they had something to do with the telescope going missing?" George asked.

"I don't know anymore," Nancy said. "But we should find them and see if they know anything—before it's too late. . . ."

Chapter

SNEAKY ON THE STAIRS

It took the girls almost twenty minutes to find the group of River Heights senior citizens. The women all had gray or white hair, and most were wearing Velcro-strapped shoes like Nancy's little cousins wore. They were huddled around the rover in the moon landing exhibit.

"This is silly," Bess said as she looked over at the group of women. Most of them had glasses hanging from chains around their necks. A few of them even walked with canes. They certainly didn't look like thieves. "There's no way one of them could've carried the telescope down the stairs."

George tucked her short brown hair behind her ears. "But maybe one of them saw something strange. You never know!"

The girls walked up to the group. Nancy pulled out the Clue Book, ready to write down everything they said. "Hi, there. We were hoping you could help us," she said. "We heard that you were on the roof of the museum between four and five p.m. today. There was a valuable telescope there that's now missing."

One of the women, a short lady wearing a pearl necklace, frowned and cupped her hand behind her ear. "What was that, dearie? You'll have to speak up!"

Nancy turned to Bess and George, who shrugged. So she repeated her words, only this time shouting them.

The lady looked confused. "A telescope? Why would we know anything about that? We sure didn't take it."

"MAYBE YOU SAW SOMETHING?" Bess asked in a loud voice. She clasped her hands together, hopeful. "DID ANYTHING SEEM ODD? DID YOU NOTICE ANYONE STRANGE ON THE ROOF WHILE YOU WERE THERE?"

"For gosh sakes, you don't have to scream!" a lady wearing a blue sweater set said in a grumpy voice. "Not all of us are deaf!" She scanned the group of women. "Where are Mildred and Susanna? They mentioned seeing something fishy on the roof."

Two women pushed forward. One was wearing glasses with dark lenses in them. The other was large and round and wore her hair in a long white braid. "That girl we saw," the one with the glasses said. "Is that what they're asking about?"

Nancy glanced sideways at George. What girl were they talking about? Was it possible they'd stumbled upon another suspect?

"What do you mean?" George asked. "You saw a girl on the roof?"

"The one with the telescope!" said the woman with the white braid. Nancy heard someone call her Mildred.

"We saw her take the telescope," the other woman, Susanna, said. "She grabbed it and walked out with us. She marched right down the stairs and out the side door."

Nancy couldn't help but smile. They had finally found a clue! "What time did that happen? Do you remember what she looked like?"

"How old was she?" Bess chimed in.

Behind them, a group of Driftwood Day Camp kids ran onto the moon exhibit. A young girl with pigtails laughed as she climbed onto the rover.

Mildred pressed her fingers to the side of her head. "Well, I think she had freckles. And maybe brown hair?"

Susanna shook her head. "No, no, no. She had pimples on her cheeks. They weren't freckles. And she had black hair, definitely black. Wasn't she tall?"

Nancy held the pen above the Clue Book, but she didn't write anything down. Susanna was wearing glasses with thick, dark lenses. Was it possible her eyesight wasn't that good?

"She wasn't tall," Mildred said. "She was average height."

Nancy looked at Bess and George. There had to be a better approach.

Bess took charge. "Okay, what do you both agree on? Did you definitely see her with the telescope?"

"Yes," they said at the same time.

Mildred ran her fingers over her long white braid. "She went down the stairs with us and out a side door. I'm certain of that."

"Me too," Susanna said. "And she had a red scarf wrapped around her head, so it was hard to see her face."

"That's right," Mildred agreed.

Nancy scribbled down the things they had both agreed on.

Suspect:
A girl:
—Red scarf
—Went down the stairs and out a side door

George studied Nancy's notes. "And how old do you think she was?"

"Forty?" Mildred said, unsure.

"No, no—she was just a teenager," Susanna said.

They both stared at Nancy, waiting for her to write something down. Nancy didn't. This happened a lot with witnesses. They would both see the same thing, but they'd see it differently. They'd give two completely different descriptions of suspects, and Nancy would have to just look for what they agreed on.

"So she's anywhere from fourteen to forty years old," Nancy said. "She was wearing a red scarf on her head and she took the telescope down the stairs and out a side door."

"Which means it could already be gone," Bess said, frowning.

"I think that scarf was a disguise!" Mildred announced.

"Maybe," Nancy said. She looked down at the Clue Book, knowing they had less than two hours before the museum closed. They had to hope the mysterious girl was still here somewhere.

George scratched her head, the way she always did when she was stumped. "What next?" she asked.

"We could walk around," Bess said. "See if we run into the girl with the red scarf."

Nancy closed the Clue Book and tucked it into her bag. She smiled, knowing there was an easier way to find her. "I think I have a better idea!"

Chapter

8

A CLUE IN A CAN

Nancy knocked on the break room door. The café was emptier than it had been before. Polly, the girl Bill liked, was clearing off a few tables. A young couple was sitting by the wall, eating bowls of soup.

When the door swung open, Alma was standing there. She ran her fingers through her red hair. "You came back!" she said. "No luck with the senior citizens from River Heights Greens?"

"That's why we're here," Nancy said. "We

think you might have video of our suspect leaving the roof."

Alma shook her head. "I told you. There are no cameras on the roof."

Bess smiled. "Actually, we're more interested in the side exit at the bottom of the stairs. Is there a security camera there?"

Alma opened the door all the way, waving the girls inside. "There is. Let's see if Paul can find the footage. Do you know when it happened?"

The girls followed Alma through the break room kitchen and into the room with all the different monitors. Paul was still there. He'd opened a bag of potato chips and now crumbs were all over the table.

"It would have been between four and five o'clock," George said. "A woman came down the stairs with the group from River Heights Greens, and then she took the telescope out a side door."

Paul hit a few buttons on his keyboard and then pulled up a picture of a stairwell. Nancy could see a door at the bottom of it. He pointed to the screen. "These are the stairs that come down from the roof, and that's the door I think you're talking about."

He hit another button and the video sped up. The clock at the bottom showed the time. 4:00 p.m., 4:05 p.m., 4:10 p.m., 4:15 p.m., 4:16 p.m., 4:17 p.m. But it wasn't until 4:46 p.m. that the video showed anyone leaving the roof.

"There!" Bess said, pointing to a few women walking down the stairs. "That's them!"

Paul slowed down the video. It showed five of the women from River Heights Greens, walking down the stairs. They all held on to the railing. Right after they passed the camera, another group came down. Mildred and Susanna were with them. A girl in a red silk scarf was there too!

"That's her!" Nancy cried. "That's exactly who Mildred and Susanna described!"

Paul pressed the pause button, and Nancy, Bess, and George studied the picture. The girl was definitely in disguise, like Mildred had said. She was hunched forward, carrying something heavy in her arms. She was wearing black pants, but the red scarf was long, and its loose ends covered most of her shirt.

"Let's see what happens," Alma said. She reached over the keyboard and hit a button. The video continued.

Once the ladies from River Heights Greens had walked offscreen, the girl stood by the door. She looked around and then opened it a crack, pulling a can from her handbag and using it to prop open the door. Then she pulled something from under her shirt. It was the telescope! She ran outside, carrying it with her.

"Why is she going outside?" George asked. "And why did she need to keep the door open?"

"There," Nancy said, pointing at the screen. "That's why."

Just beyond the door they could see a car parked at the curb. Bess smiled. "She was bringing it to someone outside the museum!"

"Which means it's probably long gone," George said with a groan.

After less than thirty seconds, the girl came back inside. The red scarf was still covering her hair and part of her face, so they couldn't see any of her features. She spun around, looking over her shoulder, and ran up the stairs. Then she jogged off camera.

"She gave the telescope to someone," Bess said. "And then she came back inside. So she could still be here somewhere."

Nancy studied the screen. She pointed to the

can that the girl had used to keep the door open. "Can you please zoom in on that can, Paul?"

Paul hit a few buttons, zooming all the way in. They looked at the can the girl had taken out of her pocket. It had a bunch of grapes on the front of it.

"Hmm . . . ," George said. "So our suspect likes grape soda."

Bess plopped down in the chair beside Paul. He offered her some potato chips, and she took a handful, snacking as she stared at the screen. "Whoever she is, she must know that Dr. Arnot has realized the telescope is gone. She must know people are looking for it."

"What do you mean?" George asked, furrowing her eyebrows.

"She left the can there," Bess said. "If she's worried about getting caught, she might come back to get it. She wouldn't want to leave evidence behind."

Alma nodded. "That's a good point. Hopefully, the soda can is still there."

"We can have a stakeout," George added.

"We'll hide nearby, waiting for her to return to the scene of the crime. The museum closes in about an hour. It's our last chance."

Paul rewound the video to the moment where the girl went out the door. Nancy stared at her face, which was completely in shadow. Who was she? What did she want with an expensive telescope? And who was the person waiting in the car outside?

Nancy crossed her arms over her chest. Hopefully, they'd get answers before it was too late.

Chapter

9

COMET-HALL CHASE

Nancy leaned forward, looking out a small, circular window. She could just barely see the side door through which the girl had taken the telescope. The soda can was still there. She was starting to put the pieces of the puzzle together. It seemed like one person in particular took that telescope. And Nancy thought she knew who that person was. She didn't want to tell Bess and George until she was sure, though.

"Do you see her?" Bess asked. She was sitting

on a bench inside the giant model of Jupiter, look-ing out the window in the planet's side. The win-dow was right where Jupiter's giant red spot was. They'd been hiding there for almost a half hour, waiting for the girl to come back.

"Not yet," George said.

On the wall inside the planet, a video played for the fourth time. "Jupiter is the fifth planet from the sun and the largest planet in the solar system," a voice blasted through the speakers. "It's a gas giant with a mass that's one-thousandth the size of our sun."

Nancy scanned the Hall of Planets. There weren't as many crowds as there had been just an hour before. A family with two small kids walked around the hall, but other than that it was empty.

"Come on," she whispered to herself as she stared at the stairwell. "Where are you?"

"Maybe she already left," George suggested as she sat down on the floor, pulling her knees to her chest.

But almost as soon as George said it, Nancy noticed a woman with a red scarf wrapped around her head come down the stairwell. The girl glanced behind her before going to the door and opening it a crack. She stared outside.

"She's here!" Nancy hissed. "It's her!"

George and Bess rushed up behind Nancy, gazing out the round window. "What is she doing?" Bess asked.

They watched the girl. She stood by the side door, peering out into the street. Every now and then she turned around, checking to make sure no one was coming down the stairs behind her.

"It's like she's waiting for someone!" Nancy turned to the entrance of the exhibit, knowing there was little time. "Come on. Now's our chance! We have to talk to her before she gets away."

Nancy ran down Jupiter's stairs and through the Hall of Planets, passing Mars and Venus. Bess and George followed close behind. When they were a few feet from the side door, the girl was turned so her back was facing them. They finally had found their suspect!

"Excuse us," Nancy said. "Can we talk to you for a minute?"

The woman straightened up. Nancy noticed she was wearing the same pants she wore in the security video. But it was only up close that Nancy saw her shiny black Mary Janes. They had a tiny apple embroidered on the side, by her toes. She'd seen the same shoes once before, earlier in the day. Any suspicions she'd had about who took the telescope were finally confirmed.

The girl paused for a moment, and then she knelt down and grabbed the soda can that propped the door open. Without saying another word, she darted past them and through the Hall of Planets.

"Hey! Wait!" Bess yelled after her.

But the girl kept going. Nancy and her friends ran through the Hall of Planets, across the museum, and into the Hall of Comets. The woman was pushing through a crowd of campers getting ready to leave. She didn't turn back—not even once.

"Hurry," George said as she picked up her pace. "We're losing her."

George was faster than Bess and Nancy, and she raced through the hall, passing the model of Halley's Comet high above. The girl with the red scarf turned down another hall that led to the museum's bathrooms. Because the museum was closing, both of the bathroom doors were locked. Their suspect was trapped!

When the girl with the red scarf realized this,

she turned around and sheepishly pulled the scarf away from her face.

"I thought so!" Nancy said. "You're the one who took Dr. Arnot's telescope!"

Bess and George stood there, frozen in shock. Could it really be?

Clue Crew—and YOU!

Can you solve the mystery of the stolen Starship 5000? Write your answers on a sheet of paper. Or just turn the page to find out!

Nancy, Bess, and George came up with three suspects. Can you think of more? Grab a sheet of paper and write down your suspects.

Who do you think took the Starship 5000? Write it down on a sheet of paper.

What clues helped you solve this mystery? Write them down on a piece of paper.

Chapter

10

A STARRY ENDING

The girl brushed her dark hair away from her face. Without the scarf, Nancy and her friends could see her glasses.

It was Kirsten Levy—Dr. Arnot's assistant!

Three important pieces of evidence had helped Nancy solve the mystery: Nancy remembered that when they first met Kirsten she'd been wearing the scarf as a headband. She'd also kept the can of grape soda she'd been drinking that morning, using it to prop open the door.

Then there were her black Mary Janes.

"I can explain," Kirsten said, her eyes filled with tears. "Please just give me a chance."

"Why would you, of all people, steal the Starship 5000?" Bess asked. "Dr. Arnot is your boss!"

Kirsten twisted the scarf around in her hands, clearly nervous. "I wasn't stealing it," she said. "That's the problem. This is all one big misunderstanding."

"What do you mean?" Nancy asked.

Kirsten let out a deep sigh. "Remember how I told you about the group project I was working on at school? Well, my partner realized the Starship 5000 would be the perfect telescope to use during the presentation. I knew Dr. Arnot would be too nervous to let me borrow it, so I decided to lend it to my friend during the hour that your group was in the planetarium show. Our school is only five minutes away, so I thought she could bring it right back."

"Right," George said, remembering what

Kirsten had told them when they'd first met her. "The Starship is the best telescope to view the Andromeda Galaxy. That's what your project was about."

Kirsten nodded. "That's right. So I lent the telescope to my friend, but her car broke down on the way back to the museum. I wasn't able to get the telescope here in time."

"So you lied about it?" George asked, crossing her arms.

Kirsten wiped her eyes. "I didn't mean to—at least not at first. It just happened. I was so scared Dr. Arnot would fire me. I was going to return it. I swear!"

"Where is it now?" Nancy asked.

Kirsten pointed behind them. "It's on its way. My friend is dropping it off any minute. That's why I was waiting by the side entrance. I'm meeting her there."

Nancy smiled at her friends. She knew Dr. Arnot wouldn't be happy that Kirsten had lied to him, but the telescope would be returned. Igor, the famous astronomer in Germany, would never even know it went missing. Wasn't that the most important thing?

Nancy turned back the way they came, waving for her friends to follow. "Let's go, then," she said. "There are only a few minutes before the museum closes. No matter what happened, Dr. Arnot will be very happy to know the Starship 5000 isn't gone forever."

Nancy and her friends stood at the bottom of the stairs, looking out the side door. It led to a street behind the museum. Kirsten sat on the bottom step, waiting for her friend.

After a few minutes a taxi pulled up. A girl with a brown ponytail stepped out, the Starship 5000 in her hands. Her skin glistened with sweat. "Kirsten!" she cried. "I'm so sorry! My car just stopped running, and I forgot my cell phone at school. I called you from the gas station I walked to."

Kirsten whispered something to her friend,

who then looked over Kirsten's shoulder at the girls. "Please—it's not Kirsten's fault," the girl said. "I was the one who wanted to use the telescope."

"I'm sure he'll just be happy to have it back," Bess said. She always seemed to feel a little bad for the suspects when they were caught.

"I'll explain it to him," Kirsten said sadly. She took the telescope from her friend and went back inside the museum, climbing the stairs to the roof. Her friend followed her, and Nancy, Bess, and George started up the steps after them. When they got to the roof the security guards were there, along with Lois and Dr. Arnot. The astronomer's face brightened when he saw the telescope. "Thank the heavens!" he cried. "You found it! Kirsten, you've saved the day! What happened? Where was it?"

Kirsten bit her lower lip. "Dr. Arnot," she began nervously. "I have to tell you something. . . ."

The man took the telescope from Kirsten's hands, holding it like a mother would hold a baby. He cradled it back and forth in his arms and petted it lovingly. Suddenly he whipped his head around and furrowed his bushy eyebrows. "What do you mean? What's wrong?"

Kirsten took a deep breath and started speaking. Her friend stood right beside her. She explained the entire story to Dr. Arnot, saying that she'd only meant to borrow the telescope for a half hour. She was going to bring it right back.

"I know I should have asked," Kirsten said. "And I shouldn't have lied when you found out it was missing. I'm so sorry that I made you so worried. I just didn't know what to do."

For the first time, Nancy noticed that Kirsten's hands were shaking. Dr. Arnot frowned, and then he finally spoke. "I'm very disappointed in you, Kirsten," he said. "And we'll have to discuss this later. But right now I'm just thankful that the telescope is back."

"It was always safe," Kirsten's friend said. "I took good care of it. If you want someone to blame, you should blame me—I asked Kirsten to take it!"

Dr. Arnot set the telescope down on the roof, adjusting it so it pointed at the sky. "Let's save the blame for some other time," he said. "There are only a few minutes before the museum is closed for the night, and I haven't seen a sky this clear and beautiful in a long time. What do you say? Should we all have a quick look at our celestial neighbors? Saturn and Venus are stunning through the scope."

That made Kirsten smile. "Thank you, Dr. Arnot," she said, dabbing her eyes.

"That would be lovely!" Lois clapped her hands

together like an excited child. Almost as soon as she said it, the other members of the astronomy club climbed the stairs to the roof, looking for them.

"You found it!" Celia cried. Marty and Hilda came up behind her. "We were wondering."

"Can I look too?" asked Trina. She stood on her tippy-toes, trying to see into the lens.

Nancy wrapped her arms around her friends, squeezing them into a tight hug as she looked up at the sky. It was a deep navy blue, with stars scattered across it like glitter. Dr. Arnot was right—it *was* beautiful.

"Good work, team," Nancy said. "We did it."

"Yes!" George said as Dr. Arnot showed Lois some stars through the telescope. "The Clue Crew cracks yet another case! And this one was out of this world!"

Test your detective skills with even more Clue Book mysteries:

Nancy Drew Clue Book #4:
Big Top Flop

Big Top Flop

ʙʏ CAROLYN KEENE • ɪʟʟᴜsᴛʀᴀᴛᴇᴅ ʙʏ PETER FRANCIS

"The best part of spring is spring break!" George Fayne said. "And the second best part is that it begins *today*!"

"The best part of spring," Bess Marvin said, "is spring *clothes*!"

Eight-year-old Nancy Drew smiled as Bess twirled to show off her new outfit. Spring clothes and spring break were awesome. And there was one more thing about spring that she and her two best friends would totally agree on. . . .

"The best part of spring is the Bingle and Bumble Circus," Nancy declared, "which is why we're here today!"

Nancy, Bess, and George *did* agree on that. Each spring the circus came to River Heights Park. This year it came with something extra fun: a junior ringmaster contest by the big circus tent!

"Don't forget the rules!" Bess said. Her long blond ponytail bounced as she spoke. "The kid who blows a whistle the longest and loudest becomes junior ringmaster on opening day tomorrow."

"How can we forget, Bess?" George asked. "We've been practicing all week."

"I whistled so loud that my puppy, Chip, ran under my bed." Nancy said.

"That's nothing!" George said, her dark eyes wide. "I whistled so loud I broke one of my mom's catering glasses!"

"How was your whistling practice, Bess?" Nancy asked.

"I stopped when I found my baby sister

sucking on my whistle," Bess said with a groan. "Gross!"

It was Friday after school, so the girls still had their backpacks. George pulled a plastic bag from hers. Inside were yellow candies shaped like lemons.

"Are those Super-Sour Suckers?" Bess asked, scrunching up her nose. "Eating those candies is like sucking lemons!"

"That's what makes them so cool!" George exclaimed. "They've got sour power!"

Nancy shook her head and said, "Sometimes I can't believe you're cousins. You two are as different as—"

"Sweet and sour?" George cut in. She was about to pop a candy into her mouth when—

"Excuse me," a boy said, "but where can a future junior ringmaster find cotton candy around here?"

Nancy, Bess, and George turned. Standing behind them was Miles Ling from the other third-grade class at school. Everyone knew that Miles wanted to be a ringmaster when he grew up. He even owned a ringmaster suit and tall black hat, which he wore today!

"You want to eat cotton candy before the contest?" Bess asked. "Won't it make your mouth too dry to whistle?"

"I don't want to *eat* the cotton candy," Miles said. "I want to stuff my ears with it!"

Nancy, Bess, and George stared at Miles.

"Stuff your ears with it?" Nancy asked slowly.

"That's how loud I whistle," Miles explained. "And when I whistle in the contest, you'll need some too!"

Nancy and her friends traded eye rolls. Miles may have been a good whistler, but he was also a very good bragger!

"We don't have any cotton candy," George said. "But you can have a Super-Sour Sucker."

George held out the bag. When Miles looked down at it his eyes popped wide open.

"N-no, thanks. . . . I've got to go," Miles blurted. He then turned quickly and disappeared in the crowd.

"Do you think Miles was serious about stuffing cotton candy in his ears?" Bess asked.

"No," George said. "But he is serious about winning the Junior Ringmaster Contest."

"Well, so are we!" Nancy said, smiling. "In fact, let's make a deal. If one of us wins, we'll bring the other two to the circus on opening night."

"Sure, we will, Nancy," Bess agreed. "After all, we're a team even when we're not solving mysteries!"

Nancy and her friends loved solving mysteries more than anything. They even had their own detective club called the Clue Crew. Nancy owned a notebook where she wrote down all her clues and suspects. She called it her Clue Book, and she carried it wherever she went.

The girls turned to gaze at the big white circus tent with red stripes. Past the tent were rows of trailers.

"That's probably where the circus people and animals stay," George pointed out. "Who are your favorites?"

Nancy smiled as she remembered the circus from last spring. "Oodles of Poodles are the best!" she said.

"I like Shirley the Seesaw Llama!" Bess said excitedly. "No one rides a seesaw like Shirley!"

"The Flying Fabuloso Family rocks!" George said. "Especially the trapeze twins, Fifi and Felix!"

"Fifi and Felix?" Bess said with a frown. "Those twins are trouble times two!"

"When they aren't on the trapeze," Nancy said, "they're playing tricks on other circus people!"

"Last year Fifi and Felix put some trick soap in Ringmaster Rex's trailer," Bess added. "His face was blue throughout the whole show!"

George shrugged and said, "The circus is all about tricks, right?"

Nancy was about to answer when the crowd began to cheer. She turned toward the tent just as Ringmaster Rex stepped out, waving his tall black hat!

"There he is!" Nancy said.

"And his face isn't blue!" Bess said with relief.

Mayor Strong and more circus people filed out of the tent. Fifi and Felix Fabuloso marched behind their parents.

"Will all kids please form a single line?" Mayor Strong asked. "Lulu the Clown is about to come around with a bag full of whistles."

The line formed lickety-split. The girls landed in the back with Miles right behind them.

"The best always goes last!" Miles bragged. "And that would be me!"

George groaned under her breath. "No wonder Miles is a good whistler," she whispered. "He's a total windbag!"

Lulu the Clown, wearing a gray wig, baggy dress, and striped stockings, walked down the line with her bag of whistles. One by one the kids reached inside and pulled out a whistle until—

"Eeeeeeeek!" a voice cried.

What happened? Nancy, Bess, and George stepped out of the line to see.

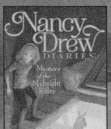